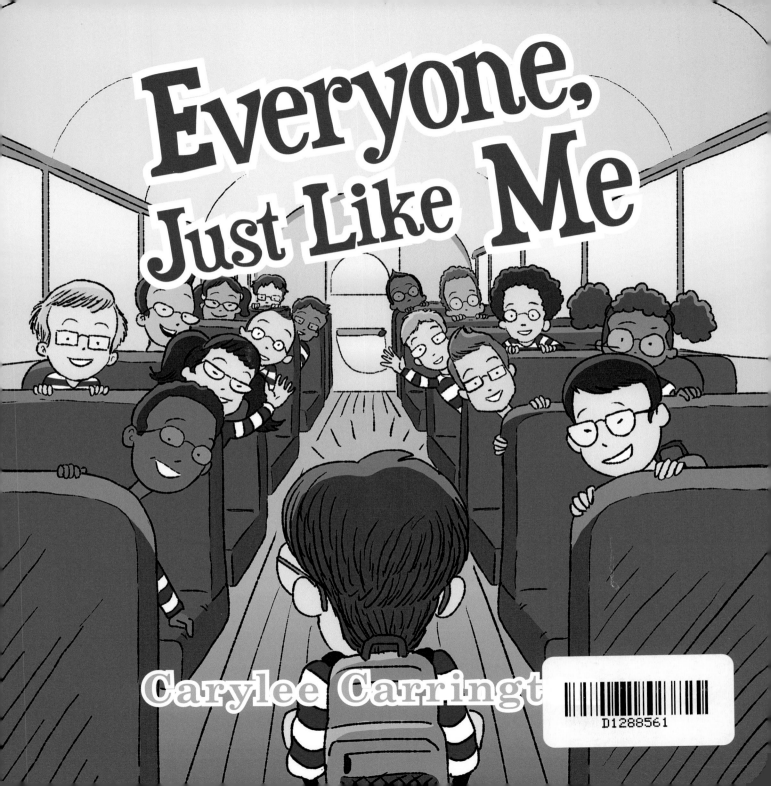

Archway Publishing books may be ordered through booksellers or by contacting:

Archway Publishing
1663 Liberty Drive
Bloomington, IN 47403
www.archwaypublishing.com
1 (888) 242-5904

ISBN: 978-1-4808-6362-0 (sc)
ISBN: 978-1-4808-6363-7 (e)

Print information available on the last page.

Archway Publishing rev. date: 08/07/2018

Joshua was feeling sad. He had to get glasses and he felt different. He would be the only one in his class with glasses. Joshua didn't like to feel different. He thought everyone would laugh at him in his new glasses, so Joshua had an idea.

That night, Joshua looked out of his window. He searched and searched for a wishing star.

Joshua found a star that twinkled brightly, and made his perfect wish. "I wish everyone was just like me". "No one will tease me now," Joshua thought.

The next morning, Joshua boarded his bus for school. To his surprise, everyone on the bus looked just like he did. And best of all, everyone wore glasses.

"Hi Joshua!" they all rang out. Joshua smiled and took a seat. Every seat was perfect he thought, because everyone is just like me.

In his class, everyone wanted the same seat---next to Chester the class fish.

At lunch everyone asked for his favorite peanut butter and banana sandwich, with a side of pickle. By the time it was his turn, there were no more bananas or pickles. All he had was a peanut butter sandwich.

At recess, everyone wanted to play on the swings, there was even a long line at the slide. Everyone wanted the same things. Though everyone was like him, Joshua started to feel alone.

That night, Joshua saw another wishing star. This time he wished to have a friend that was not so much like him.

The next day, Joshua went to school and saw his friend Caleb and thought, "This is great. Caleb isn't just like me, I can sit next to him in class."

But everyone else, who was still just like Joshua, thought the same thing.

Everyone wanted to sit next to Caleb at lunch and they all wanted to play with him at recess.

Having everyone wanting to play with him, Caleb thought, was just too much, so Caleb decided to play alone.

That night, Joshua peered out his bedroom window searching for a wishing star, but it was cloudy and it was hard to find any star in sight.

Just as he was about to give up, he saw a clear spot and a little twinkle in the sky. He thought, "a little twinkle, for my big wish."

"I wish that everyone was not just like me. Make everyone different, special and unique."

The next morning, as he boarded the school bus, he was excited to see that everyone was different. He said "hello!" to everyone, with a big smile.

In class, he took his favorite seat next to Chester the class fish.

At lunch, he was able to get his favorite peanut butter and banana sandwich, and he even got an extra pickle.

At recess, he played on the swings and there were no lines at the slide. He played with Caleb and even lead a pony ride.

Best of all, no one teased Joshua about his glasses. Joshua saw that all his friends were different, and he was happy with that. Everyone is different and special in their own way.

About the Author

Carylee Carrington is a new author who lives in Northern Virginia. When not writing, she enjoys tackling DIY projects, keeping fit, and running around with her two boys.